First Ballet

by Deanna Caswell
illustrated by Elizabeth Matthews

Disney • HYPERION BOOKS / NEW YORK

For Callie—D.C.

To Gabe—E.M.

For information address Disney · Hyperion Books, 114 Fifth Avenue, New York, New York 10011-5690.
First Edition
10 9 8 7 6 5 4 3 2 1
Printed in Singapore
ISBN 978-1-4231-1353-9
Reinforced binding
Library of Congress Cataloging-in-Publication Data on file
Visit www.hyperionbooksforchildren.com

Sun sets. Shoes shine.
Sunday best. Stand in line.

Hands entwined in the cold.
First ballet. Five years old.

Crisp air. Breath clouds.
Precious ticket. Eager crowds.

Murmurs, whispers. Velvet seat.
Clutching program. Swinging feet.

Lights dim. Curtains rise.
Hushed lips. Watchful eyes.

Single dancer on the boards.
Flutes and strings. Lilting chords.

Satin slippers. Dainty dress.
Polished movements. Poised finesse.

Pirouette and small jeté.

Arabesque and grand plié.

Dazzled gasp, so surprised.
Dreamy gaze, mesmerized.

Sweet enchantment. Story grows.
A dream unfolds on pointed toes.

Graceful spins. Lifted chins.
Swift hands tickle violins.

Daring jumps. Heart thumps.
Music swells. Goose bumps.

Hours pass as dancers float.
Story closes. Final note.

Bow and curtsy. Audience stands.
Roses falling. Clapping hands.

Curtains lower. Houselights gleam.
Crowd awakens from the dream.

Happy faces, sharing smiles.
Cheerful chatting in the aisles.

Gather coats and bundle tight.
Warm cheeks greet the chilly night.

The spell is broken. Clocks chime.
Wave good-bye until next time.

Twirling home. Sway and prance.
Captivated by the dance.